The Fall

by

Anthony McGowan

D0168553

To the pupils and teachers of Corpus
Christi High School 1976-1981, and
particularly Margaret Freeman, the best
and the kindest.

First American edition published in 2012 by Stoke Books,
an imprint of Barrington Stoke Ltd

18 Walker Street, Edinburgh, United Kingdom, EH3 7LP

www.stokebooks.com

Copyright © 2011 Anthony McGowan

A catalog record for this book is available from
the US Library of Congress

Distributed in the United States and Canada by Lerner Publisher
Services, a division of Lerner Publishing Group, Inc.

241 First Avenue North, Minneapolis, MN 55401

www.lernerbooks.com.

ISBN 978-1-78112-094-1

Printed in China

Contents

PART 1

DUFFY

Chapter 1
School

My friend, Neil Johnson, just called. He was at school with me in England, but I hadn't heard from him in a long time – not since I moved to the United States. His number wasn't even in my cell phone. I didn't know who it was till he said his name. Then he got straight down to it.

"Is that Mog?" he said. Nobody had called me Mog since I was at school. "Have you heard?"

"Heard what?" I said.

"Rush."

"Chris Rush?"

"Yeah," Neil said.

"What about him?" I remembered Chris. He was at school with us too.

"He's dead."

And that was it. It was like a time machine. Suddenly, I was back in England, in the old school, years ago.

Corpus Christi High School, what a heap that was. The kids were mainly crazy. Even the teachers were crazy. Their first job was to scare you, and only when you were really scared would they try to teach you stuff. Maybe not all of them were like that, but sometimes it seemed that way.

And you didn't have to do that much to get on the wrong side of them. A teacher might not like the look on your face, or how you talked, or how you sat at your desk. Some would scream at you till your face was covered in hot breath and spit. Some would play mind games – they would embarrass you in front of your friends to make it look as if there was something weird about you, so everyone treated you like a freak.

The teachers always seemed to pick on the weaklings, not the nutters, or the big, meat-headed bullies, with fists like blocks of stone, and bodies bursting like the Incredible Hulk out of their school uniforms.

Mind you, you can't really blame them. They must have been scared of some of the Corpus kids. Who wouldn't be?

There was one called Gaz Manson. He had a sort of baby face, and he always looked as if he was smiling. But he had a streak of pure evil in him. He'd come out of nowhere in the school yard and dead leg you so you could hardly walk, never mind fight back. And then he'd loom over you and not even punch you, but slap your face, just because it was the most embarrassing thing he could do to you, as if you were a little kid or a girl.

He ruled the school until Terry Coleman turned up, fresh out of Juvenile Detention. The two of them stared each other down for a few days. They both had kids hanging on to them, like the fish that stick on the bottom of sharks. But you could see Gaz's gang leak away. It was like an old man losing his teeth.

You could understand why. It was because Coleman was such a monster. Just looking at him made you want to wet your pants. He had this great big head, and these massive jaws and teeth like a cannibal or something. And his fists. They were like a man's fists, not a kid's.

In the end, Gaz and Terry had their fight. They went at it on our all-weather sports pitch. Big laugh that, by the way, that the school called it an 'all weather' pitch. It was made out of some sort of red gravel, and it was only an all-weather pitch in so far as it was crap in all weathers. When it rained it was this thick, sticky mud, and when it was dry, it was like sand-paper.

You could tell it was all over for baby-face Manson before the fight even started. He must have had some guts under all that blubber even to try to fight. If it had been me I'd have turned around and gone on running till I reached a fence I couldn't climb over or a sea I couldn't swim. But Gaz waited for his doom. It didn't take long. He put his fists up, like a real fighter, but Coleman just bashed him a few times, like he was hammering in a fence post.

Then, when Gaz was lying there, moaning and drooling, Coleman grabbed his hair and rubbed his face into the red gravel. It was like he was grating cheese. You could hear Gaz saying "please, please," but Coleman only stopped when he got bored with it.

There was a girl from 7th grade there, and she puked.

It was shocking, even to us. There was a big crowd watching, the way there always is for a fight. It's not like there was much else exciting going on. But we weren't shouting and yelling and laughing like you normally do when there's a fight. We were just sort of standing there, kind of embarrassed.

Then that girl puked and it smelled rank. It made you want to be somewhere else.

And then it got even worse, even if this bit does sound sort of funny. Coleman somehow got a pork pie. I don't even know how. It was suddenly just in his hand. A pork pie, for God's sake. Back in England we ate these all the time. Maybe it was Gaz's lunch, and Coleman took it out of his pocket or something. Anyway, Coleman got the pork pie and he mashed it into Gaz's face. The jelly and the pink, fatty meat. He rubbed it into Gaz's face which was already a mess from the red gravel. OK, it *was* kind of funny. And we did laugh. But it was a weird sort of laughing, and it wasn't that far away from crying.

After the fight we didn't know if we should be cheering or shaking. We'd all been scared of Gaz, but at least we knew what he was like. And he was fat – we could all outrun him. That's why he had to do that dead-legging thing, so you couldn't run.

Coleman was different. He was big but he wasn't fat. He was all muscle, big and tough. I know Gaz was evil but he was *our* bully. We didn't know Coleman. He was new. It was like they say – "better the devil you know".

In fact it turned out alright. Coleman wasn't really bothered with us. He didn't really notice us. It was like he was a lion and we were some little animals that weren't worth the effort of eating. Rabbits or something. He was after bigger prey – high schoolers, the rulers of other schools, local hard cases. Big meat.

And the *really* funny thing is that it even worked out OK for Gaz. Now he wasn't the big bully any more, he relaxed a bit, and it turned out he was good at art and stuff like pottery. Go figure.

So, that's the teachers and the kids. The school we all swilled around in was just right for us. From the outside, Corpus looked like some sort of a factory. Maybe where meat gets made into dog food. Something grim, anyway. Everything about it was gray. Gray concrete, gray asbestos. The only color came from the graffiti. And even the graffiti was crap – nothing funny, nothing clever, just dirty pictures and soccer stuff.

All in all, there may have been worse schools in our town, but not many. The other schools hated playing us at soccer. They were scared of us. We were the place their kids got expelled to, and God help them when they got to us.

Chapter 2
The Beck

Next to the school there was a stream that we called the beck. Then there was a field, called the Gypsy Field. It was called that because Gypsies would camp there, but you'd never know when, and you'd never know for how long. Beyond the field there was a run-down neighborhood where most of the kids lived.

The beck wasn't like some country stream, or a stream in a story, full of fish and tadpoles and stuff, sparkling with white water. It was brown and oily. It stank like an outhouse on a campsite. Nothing lived in it, except for the rats and green scum that could dissolve strollers and dead dogs. Didn't matter. For us it was a place of adventure, danger. A place where things happened.

The 'us' was the group of kids I used to mess around with. Nerds and misfits, mainly. Most of us got picked on by the bullies because we had big lips, or curly hair, or satchels instead of Adidas sports bags. This was all before Coleman took over from Gaz Manson as the guy you had to be scared of.

Chris Rush hung out with me and my friends. I don't know why. He wasn't really one of us. I mean he wasn't nerdy. He was pretty cool. He was into all the right bands. And he was tough without being a meat-head. Chris was short, but both times I saw him fight he destroyed bigger kids. He could go straight from normal, cheery Chris into mad fight mode, with hot fire in his eyes. His thin body would shake with this mad power he had, where he could feel no pain.

Well, actually I think I do know why Chris hung out with us. It was because of me. He liked me. We just clicked. We got each other's jokes, we felt easy together. He came to stay at my house, sleeping in my brother's bed while he was off elsewhere. We went shoplifting together, and then gave what we stole – pens, CDs, comics, whatever – to the homeless, or girls we liked. Sometimes we just threw our loot into the beck and watched it bubble down into the scum.

Chris was brainy, but he didn't do any homework. He read books, sometimes, which not many of us did. He talked about a book called *Animal Farm*, where the animals took over the world, but then messed it up for themselves by turning into people. Stuff like that.

I feel a bit weird about saying this next bit, but I've got to or you won't understand what I'm going to tell you. You see, the thing about Chris, the truly *special* thing about Chris, was that he was good. Good like he wanted other people to be happy, and if they weren't, then he wasn't either. He was the only kid I ever saw genuinely take a chance and stick up for another person in a way that could have got him beaten up, or even humiliated. You could sort of feel the goodness coming off him. Even when he was fighting, or stealing stuff from shops, he was still *good*.

His goodness was why he let Duffy come into our lives.

Duffy was really uncool. He was a boring, pale kid with gray teeth and skinny legs. He had no jokes, no talk, no style, and no real brains. He was a zero, a hole in the shape of a kid.

But Duffy had a big problem. His fatal flaw was having a mother who loved him. One day, early on in 7th grade, so he was eleven or twelve, his mom dropped him off in front of the school. They had a crappy car but that wasn't a problem. It was what she did that killed him. I don't mean killed his body, but killed his soul. Because there, with a school yard full of wolves and hyenas and jackals looking on, she kissed him, leaving the mark of a set of bright red lips on his white cheek.

She might as well have stabbed him in the heart with a screwdriver.

'Cos from then on it was open season. Duffy got punched and kicked by anyone who felt like it, which turned out to be almost everybody. The one or two people who didn't bother hitting him ignored him. No one ever simply teased him, because that way he could have joined in with the joke, and we didn't want that.

Gaz Manson was his particular tormentor.

Duffy would be standing on his own in a corner of the school yard, trying to be invisible. Gaz and his friends would spot him. They'd fan out to make sure he couldn't run for it – and then walk over.

"Right then, Duffers, you faggot, give us your money," Gaz would say. Then he'd add, "Your mom's not here to kiss you now."

Duffy would pay up, never saying a word.

Sometimes Gaz would leave it at that. More often he and his friends would line up in twos. Then they'd make Duffy run between them, and they'd punch and kick him from both sides. Sometimes they'd just take it in turns to whack him, punching the top of his arm until he cried. You hoped he would cry because then the bullying stopped, but you also felt his shame, and you wanted him to hold out.

Two years of that and Duffy was more like a ghost than ever. He didn't want anyone to notice him. He'd slip from classroom to classroom without a word. If he had any feelings, he kept them tightly locked up inside him and made sure nothing showed on his face.

Some of us should have seen him, should have helped him. But then we might have been infected with what he had – a deathly, ghostly stink that attracted the bullies, like demons coming to drag him into Hell, where they would punch and kick him for their sport.

Chapter 3
Duffy and Chris

It all began when Chris let Duffy eat his sandwich near us at lunch. There were five of us: Neil Johnson, the O' Connells, Chris and me, and we always ate our sandwiches in the same place – up by the school wall. It was fun. We used to mess around with each other, but in a friendly way, like you do. Pete O' Connell had this thing he did. If you chewed up your sandwich and spat it out, he'd eat it. Benny O' Connell had the opposite trick. He could make himself puke without putting his fingers down his throat. Johnson didn't do much, but he smiled a lot and everyone liked him.

Chris was the center of it all. He started all the jokes, and if anyone said anything that was meant to be funny, we'd all look at Chris to see if he was laughing. If he was, then we laughed too.

It was OK. And having Chris there meant that Gaz and his lot left us alone. But we knew we were never totally safe. It wouldn't take much for the bullies to notice us.

So, one day, Duffy came and sat near us. He didn't try to sit right beside us, but he was kind of close, so it looked as if he was one of us.

On another day, we might have thrown stones at Duffy like a dog and driven him away, but Chris started talking to him. Nothing much, just chatting. Music maybe, as if Duffy would know anything. TV shows, as if we cared what Duffy thought about them. Girls, like he had a chance. Before the rest of us knew what was happening he was sitting with us and we didn't look so cool any more.

I can't remember now if I spoke to him at all then, or in the next few weeks as he began to tag along with us. I can't remember any of what was said, just our groans as he tried to become one of us. He was so eager to please and just to be with us. It was always Chris who let him join in and made room for him.

I didn't like it. It made me feel kind of sick inside. And now, when I look back I can see the sick feeling had two parts to it. The biggest thing was that I was scared Duffy was going to make us a target for the bullies. I was scared we'd catch his death-stink and that we'd end up like him.

The other part of the sick feeling was smaller but worse. When I think about it now I'm ashamed. I was jealous. Jealous of Chris and Duffy. I don't mean ... well, you know. Nothing like that. I just mean that Chris was my best friend, and now this other kid was getting in between us, and I didn't understand why.

Then Chris told Duffy he could come after school to hang out by the beck.

That made me feel even more sick. Jumping the beck was the most fun we had.

Most of the beck was too wide to jump. The muddy banks were slippery and steep. You had to be nuts to risk falling into that rank water, half rat piss, half shit. Two or three times I tried to jump and fell in. When I got home I got a smack from Mom when she got a whiff of me.

But there were two or three spots where the beck was narrow and not too slippery. You could jump it with a good chance of a safe landing.

And so jumping the beck was one of the things that you did, in your little gangs, once every few weeks after school. If you did it more often than that, it would make it less exciting. As it was, it was awesome. You got that feeling of freedom as you jumped. Nothing holding you. Nothing tying you down. Just you and the air. Then there was the joy when you landed safe with your friends around you. True, they might chuck stones at the water as you jumped to try to splash you so it looked like you'd wet yourself, but they were on your side. We were all together against the beck, against the mud, against the water, against the world.

Of course Duffy had never been one of the beck jumpers. It wasn't a place for loners. One evening, when I was on the bus, I thought I saw him down by the beck, on his own. He was looking into the water. Maybe he was dreaming of flying across and then friends clapping him on the back and cheering. I wished that he had friends of his own to do stuff with.

But now he was with us, laughing at our jokes.

"What do you call a fly with no wings?"

"Dunno."

"A walk."

"Ha."

"What do you call a fly with no wings and no legs?"

"Dunno."

"A raisin!"

"Ha ha."

"How do you know when you're really ugly?"

"Dunno."

"Dogs close their eyes while they're humping your leg."

"Ha ha ha."

We were getting all worked up, like we always did before we went jumping. Adrenaline pumping.

We got to the easy bits. I made a jump, but it wasn't good. I didn't land in the beck or anything, but it wasn't ... *great*. It didn't have that way about it that made people go still for a few seconds and then cheer.

Then Duffy had a go. He looked stupid, of course, flapping like a bird that's fallen out of the nest. But Chris caught his hand at the far side and pulled him home when he looked like sinking back into the mud.

I didn't like it. It felt like Chris had put a hand into my guts and pulled something out.

Chris was my friend, and he was spending more time talking to Duffy than me. Duffy didn't swear, had nothing to say and looked like a geek. Why would Chris want him as a friend?

"What's up, Mog?" someone said. Johnson, I think. Not Chris. Chris didn't care. Chris was too busy looking after Duffy.

"Nothin," I grunted.

Then whoever it was – Johnson, or maybe Pete O' Connell, I can't remember – just went off, and didn't bother asking me again.

I was going to go home.

And then I remembered the refrigerator.

Chapter 4
The Refrigerator

At one of the beck's widest, deepest parts, there was a sort of a pool. Not as nice as the word "pool", would make you think. The water was scummy, and it stank. And that's where the Gypsies had dumped a refrigerator. At least I think it was the Gypsies, but they always got the blame for stuff like that, whether or not it was them.

Anyway, this refrigerator looked like a sunken ship, with only a small diamond shape of deck showing above the water. No one had ever jumped over the pool before – you'd need to be some kind of Olympic champion to do it. But I was thinking that with the refrigerator there, maybe a kid could jump from the right-hand bank, land with one foot on the refrigerator and then take off again, and land safely on the left bank. The distance was OK, but you'd need clever footwork and good eyes and the refrigerator would have to be stuck deep in the mud to take your weight.

I knew the refrigerator wasn't stuck in the mud.

I knew it wasn't because I'd poked it with a stick. It had wobbled. The refrigerator wasn't sitting right in the mud at the bottom of the beck. It was balancing on something – a brick or some other garbage. Bike, iron, dead dog. It only needed a little push and the refrigerator would shift. Anyone jumping onto it would fall, and that meant landing in scum up to your balls.

So now I edged up to Duffy. I think it was the first time I spoke to him.

"There's a cool place to jump," I said. "Up at the pool. You have to steppy-stone on the

refrigerator. It's not hard – I've done it.
Chris'll think it's awesome."

I showed Duffy the pool. The others had
found a dead rat and were kicking it around.

"Is it safe?" Duffy wanted to know.

His voice hadn't broken and he spoke like a
girl. I laughed, mocking his timidity.

"Course it is," I said.

I could see what he was thinking. Half of
him was scared of falling. The other half
wanted to be one of us. He was thinking that if
he did the jump, he could be in our gang. He'd
be cool. All the years of being sad and lonely
would be over. He'd have friends, people to be
with. People on his side when he got punched.
People he could talk about when his mom
asked him how school was today. What had he
said to her over the past two years? Had he
made up friends, told her stories about made-
up games and jokes? Or had he just looked
down at his plate and had to put up with the
shame? "Mom, there's no one. I'm alone."

He looked up at me.

"OK." He grinned but I could tell he was nervous.

"Duffy's jumping the refrigerator," I screamed at the others, so he didn't have time to change his mind.

Johnson and the O' Connells cheered, and came running. Chris looked a bit worried, and came more slowly.

"What fo'?" he said. "Did you tell him to?"

"It were his idea," I said.

Duffy looked at me. *Was I trying to make him look good?* he was thinking.

He said, "Dunt look too bad."

Chris said, "I wunt."

Johnson and the O' Connells shouted at him to go on. They had nothing to lose, whatever happened.

Duffy took off his jacket and gave it to me. He had six or seven pens in the pocket, and a clean folded handkerchief, and some money. A fiver and some coins.

Chris was telling him what to do.

"Don't take a long run," he said. "Just a few steps. You've got to get the aim right. As soon as your foot hits the refrigerator, you've got to jump off again, or you'll be stranded."

Chris and Duffy were standing close together. Duffy was as close as he could get to Chris, nodding. He looked happy for the first time since his mother had kissed him two years before.

Chris went along the bank to an easy place to cross, jumped, and then walked back along the other side to help Duffy land. The rest of us stayed on this bank. Duffy got ready. He went up to the edge of the water, back two steps, up to the water again, and then back for the last time.

He jumped.

It was a good jump – almost perfect – high and fast. He would hardly need to put his foot on the refrigerator to get over to the other side.

I couldn't see his face, because we were behind him, but I'm sure he was smiling. He'd left all the bad stuff behind, the years of horror, the beatings, the dog mess rubbed on his blazer, all that. It was like he was a butterfly shaking off its dry, brown cocoon and becoming beautiful.

I remember our biology teacher, Mr. Wells, who was alright for a teacher, told us about the eye one day. He told us that the message in the light gets sent to your brain, so you could say that you don't see with your eye, but with your brain.

That was all OK, but then he went a bit crazy and started talking about seeing things with your brain, not your eye. He said when you see something in the world with your brain, your brain goes out into the world. Like if you watch a rocket go off in the sky, the place where you see it isn't your eye or even your brain, but up there, in the middle of the sky, with the colors showering all around you.

I was seeing Duffy's face in my brain. All smiles and happy at last. And I was with him, in the air over the beck.

And then Duffy's foot came down on the refrigerator and the refrigerator let him down, just like I had planned. The refrigerator rocked, and Duffy fell with a splash into the water, his face all shocked and scared. His face told me something else too – that he knew that I had done it, and that I had meant to do it.

Neil and the O' Connells fell laughing to their knees. This was the funniest thing they'd ever seen.

"Straight in, head first," Neil crowed.

"Did you see his face?" the O' Connells shouted.

"Classic. Was that your idea, Mog?" Neil asked.

"Genius," the O' Connells said.

"You knew, didn't you?" said Neil again.

"Freaking awesome." That was the O' Connells.

We didn't even look as Duffy dragged himself out of the beck. But I noticed an odd thing. Chris didn't help him. He just stood there and looked and his face was blank. Then he walked away, back across the rough Gypsy Field to the neighborhood where he lived.

We went around and met up with Duffy. He tried to laugh with the others.

"My mom'll kill me!"

But Duffy didn't look at me as he took his jacket back from me.

I'd taken the fiver from his pocket. I don't know why.

Afterwards, Duffy walked up to the bus stop. He didn't ever try and sit with us again at lunchtime, and Chris didn't ask him.

I don't think that the beck did Duffy too much harm. I pray that it is so. There's a blank in my memory but I have a feeling that he found some other friends like himself. The bullying must have stopped, because it always does, if you wait for long enough.

But none of that takes away my shame. Duffy was just like us, just like us except that his mother once kissed him on the cheek, and that kiss did him in. Then I'd betrayed him because I was jealous.

And I knew all that even then. The next day I gave the fiver to a homeless man and it was like I'd given away a knife I used to kill someone.

After that I made myself forget Duffy, and what I'd done, because if I didn't, how could I get through another day?

PART 2

THE CROSS-BOW

Chapter 5
The Psycho Brother

After Duffy, things changed between Chris and me. It was hard to say just what had changed. We were still friends, sort of, but not in the same way. When we met up he wouldn't look at me – he'd look at something somewhere in the distance. Before, we'd got each other's jokes without having to explain anything, but now there was a little space there.

The click had gone.

And he didn't bother with the others any more. He never sat with us at lunch time. He would just nod to us. It was as if he'd done his bit, seen it as a waste of time, and moved on.

Looking back now, I can see that Chris himself was already beginning to change, on the way to becoming that other Chris, the one I couldn't know. Before, it was as if there were many different roads ahead of him, but now there was only one, and it wasn't a good road.

But he still wasn't like his brother, Kevin. Kevin was a thug, plain and simple. A thug and a thief. He was sly and mean. And stupid. Every time he saw Chris he'd take his money off him, then hit him, or get him in a head lock, or just throw him down. It was how he got laughs from his thug friends.

There was one good thing about Kevin, and one good thing only – he had a cross-bow. Chris used to talk about it all the time, how you could kill stuff with it.

Chris couldn't think about anything except the cross-bow and so nor could I. Maybe it was because nobody had any guns, back then. And this cross-bow was the nearest thing to a gun there was.

It was deadly and we couldn't get our hands on it, and so it called to us with a voice like honey.

Once, we were hanging out in Chris's back yard. It was full of broken bits of engine that his dad was going to fix up to sell one day. But it looked like junk to me, and anyway his dad was always drunk on the sofa, watching TV.

I needed to go to the bathroom. On the way I had to go past Kevin's bedroom. Most of the time he kept it locked, but this time the door was open. The cross-bow was hung up on the wall, the way some people had crosses. I couldn't stop looking at it.

Next thing I knew my face was smashed up against the wall. Kevin had come up behind me. My legs were dangling. I couldn't breathe.

"Ever touch that and you're dead," said Kevin, his voice cold and calm. "Get it?"

I tried to say something, but nothing came out, so I nodded.

Then Kevin spat in my ear and threw me down the stairs.

Outside Chris looked at me.

"We'll get it," he said. "One day."

Chapter 6
Got It

And he was right. The thing we'd been praying for happened. Kevin was caught stealing one too many times, and got sent to a Juvenile Detention center fifty miles away.

A day later Chris came to our back door. Like I said, Chris had already begun to change then, and my mom didn't really like me hanging around with him.

"I've got it," he said, softly. And I knew what he meant.

We'd got the cross-bow. It was ours. And we knew what we were going to do with it.

For years we'd talked of hunting the rats that were all over the beck. You could even see them from the third floor in the science classroom at school. They used to perch on that same dumped refrigerator, the one I tricked Duffy with. The rats stood out against the white. An easy shot, we thought. Chris had been saving up for an air rifle, nicking pens and watches to sell at school. But the cross-bow was better than a pellet gun. Oh, yes.

"Got to be early, meet you tomorrow at five, under the bridge," he said.

There was no messing around this time. This was serious.

"OK."

I didn't sleep at all that night. All I could think about was the hunt. I kept trying to see it in my head, but I couldn't get the pictures right. All I had was the feelings. Excitement, danger, the need to kill. And I thought this was the time that me and Chris would be together again, like the old days. We'd got rid of the others, scraped them off our shoes like dog mess. Just me and him, now.

And the cross-bow.

I slipped out of the house and into the morning, before the dawn. It was February, and the air was thick with cold. Like you could cut a slice and eat it. And I wished you could have eaten the cold, because I'd had no breakfast.

The bridge Chris was talking about was just a little foot-bridge over the beck. People used to meet under it to sniff glue or smoke pot. He was waiting for me. He was holding a black trash bag, its contents heavy, lumpy, awkward.

"Is that it?" I said and pointed at the bag. Stupid question.

Chris just nodded. There was a time when he'd have joked about me asking such a dumb question, and we'd have laughed about it together. But not any more. Didn't matter. We had other things to think about now.

He peeled back the bag, and held it out for me to see.

Here it was, at last, the cross-bow. Wood, worn smooth; steel, bright and springy; wire so tight it looked like you could play it like a harp.

My God but it was beautiful.

"You do this," he said, and he put his foot in a sort of metal hook at the end of it and pulled hard at the bow string. A click. And then Chris slotted a bolt in the groove. The bolt was only about six inches long, but it was heavy and looked deadly.

"Cost five pounds each, these bolts. Don't lose 'em or he'll know what we've done and kill us when he's out."

"Can I hold it?" I asked.

He looked at me, his eyes showing nothing.

"No," he said.

Then he walked, and I went with him along the mud path that ran along beside the beck. The walk was half a mile and we were two hunters and did not say a word. The thrill of death was on us.

It was almost religious, as if we were involved in some ancient rite. A sacrifice.

And it was nearly beautiful in that place at that time. There was a low mist on the Gypsy Field. The sky was light in the east, but there were still some stars.

I thought I saw something move. At first I thought it was a rat, and I touched Chris on the arm. But it was too big. Too big and too beautiful.

"Fox," said Chris.

It was sniffing around some garbage left by the Gypsies. Like I said, you'd never know when the Gypsies were going to come or when they were going to leave. One morning you'd wake up to see caravans and junk. A horse with long shaggy hair growing over its hooves like tattered flared trousers. A stroller. A deck-chair. Buckets. Bits and pieces. Loose stuff, the things you'd get by shaking our town and seeing what fell out. And always the ashes of a fire, not fire itself; the burnt-out end of everything.

It always freaked us out a bit when the Gypsies were there. The Gypsy kids would line up, outside the school fence, and look at us. Their fingers were like birds' claws, poking through the wire. They weren't curious. They never shouted at us or even said anything. Just stared.

The hard kids in the school who should have stared back were scared. They'd find other things to do at the far end of the school yard. These thin faces, skull-shaved, the tang of old smoke hanging over them, were too weird for them.

I remember someone saying, "They call us *meat*."

It made the hairs stand up on my neck.

But the Gypsies would go as suddenly and silently as they came. This time they'd left bags of trash and that was what the fox had found.

You wouldn't think an animal that eats garbage would be beautiful. But in the dawn light the fox flickered like flame. I could see the white around its nose, and then the black lips, and the tongue that seemed to hang out too far. But it was the deep red of its back that you noticed. A red not like blood, or like any red thing you could think of, but like the color turned into a feeling. It was like what that teacher had said about your brain going out there into the world when you see something. I was out there with the fox. I felt its fur in my face, I breathed it in. My fingers stroked the white neck and then swept up to feel the soft ears.

Chris threw half a brick. The fox didn't run at once, like you'd expect. Instead it tensed, looked at us, thought, and then melted away. And I thought I tasted its smell in the air. Not soft, like its fur looked, but harsh and a little cruel.

"Come on," said Chris.

And on we went.

Chapter 7

Hunter

I can hear the sounds still, the sounds we made as we picked our way along the bank – the flapping of our pants, the nylon scratch of parka on parka, the sucking of the mud, the first car horns from Selby Road, that sounded like far away cows.

The fox had made the morning perfect. It was a wild thing. A killer. Like us. This wasn't our town. This wasn't now. We could have been ten thousand years ago. We could have been the heroes of our tribe.

Chris's hand came up.

We were there.

We could just see the white of the sunken refrigerator. Chris turned and pointed to the earth. "Down."

We squatted there, two toads on the bank.

And we waited for the rats to come.

Those first minutes showed me what it meant to be alive. I could hear each blade of grass move, smell the mud at the bottom of the beck, see the dew on a spider's web a hundred feet away.

But as the minutes went by, and the rats stayed in their holes, I became myself again. A boy squatting in the cold by a dirty stream.

Chris yawned.

I had some chocolate. Chris some cigarettes. He passed me one, lit from a stolen lighter. I prayed I wouldn't choke, and swallowed smoke deep into my guts. It was Chris who taught me to smoke, and I didn't want to let him down.

Slowly the town came awake around us. We heard a milk van along the street next to the field, the bottles chinking together. The first bus. One or two cars.

Chris held the cross-bow all the time, his thumb rubbing against the grain of the wood. I'd never seen him like this before. To me the cross-bow was a cool weapon, an adventure, but for him it was something more. Did it mean he was free from Kevin at last? Was it power in his hands?

I badly wanted to try the cross-bow, but I knew that I was lucky just to be there with Chris, and I didn't want to push it.

At last, when it was nearly time to go back home to get ready for school, Chris said, "Here," and gave me the cross-bow.

At the time I thought it was Chris being his old self. Like when he was kind and wanted to make other people happy. The way he was before I did what I did to Duffy and that changed things. Now I don't think it was that. I think he'd just given up on the rats.

But none of that mattered then. I had the cross-bow. God, it was superb. I'd never felt anything so perfect before. I knew it would only be mine for a few minutes, but that made it all the more precious. I could feel the power of the thing in my hands.

I badly wanted to pull the trigger and fire the bolt, to feel the kick of it, to watch the bolt arc away. But I couldn't just let it fly, not after what Chris had said about losing the bolts.

The sky was all light now, and the sun was edging up the sky. Still no rats.

"I need to piss," said Chris, and unzipped himself.

I thought he'd turn away and do it against the bank. But he didn't. He faced out into the beck, and sent his piss bending high over the water.

And at that exact moment, the sun rose from the earth. Its light caught Chris and turned him into a shadow.

But then something magical happened.

Through the high arc of his piss, there was a rainbow. The color shone in the air like a kingfisher. It was like the experiment with a glass prism we did in science, when we split white light into strands of color. And again, like Mr. Wells said, my mind was out in the rainbow, and not the rainbow in my mind.

"Look, look," said Chris, his voice crackling with the joy of it.

Back then, I thought it was the rainbow he was laughing at. But now, I think that it couldn't have been the rainbow. Only I could have seen that because the sun had to be shining through the stream at the right angle, and if the angle was right for me, it would have been wrong for Chris.

So maybe he was just laughing at how he was pissing from bank to bank and not at the rainbow he'd made.

But still he laughed, and then grinned, and he was the old Chris again.

Then, as he put himself away, his face changed.

"Watch it," he said, his voice sharp.

I was pointing the cross-bow right at him.

"Sorry."

I felt embarrassed, a fool. He'd been right not to trust me with the deadly thing.

Chapter 8
Killer

And then I saw the fox again, tracking across the Gypsy Field. It seemed to walk on its tip-toes, like a dancer. I guessed it was going back to its hole, now that the day was here, and its belly full of scraps.

But it stopped, fifty feet away, and began to pull at something in the grass.

It hadn't seen us because we were down in the cutting made by the beck, and the stink of the scummy pool hid our smell.

And then I felt the cross-bow call to me. It wanted me to fire it, the way a girl wants you to kiss her. I couldn't resist.

"Watch this," I said to Chris.

I meant to fire the bolt way in front of the fox. So that the fox saw it. I wanted to see the fox look up in surprise, see us, and then trot away on tip-toes again. I wanted it to look at me and include me in its world.

I hefted the cross-bow to my shoulder. It was like holding up a sleeping child because it was so heavy. I closed my eyes. I felt the kick of the cross-bow as I pulled the trigger.

Just before I closed my eyes, I think I'd seen Chris put out his hand to stop me.

I didn't stop.

There was no sound. No *thlup* as the bolt went home; no whine or yelp from the fox.

But the cross-bow bolt hit the fox in the neck, and sent the animal rolling back into the long grass.

Silence first, and then I found that I was laughing, a nervous, high laugh.

Chris grabbed the cross-bow from my hands, and we both ran over to the fox. The bolt had gone through its windpipe. The fox was moving its legs. Brown eyes looked up at us as if the fox was trying to understand what had happened. It was still scared and it tried to twist away from us. But the bolt had pinned its throat and all the fox could do was move round it on the ground.

"You'll have to kill him now," said Chris.

It was about then that I started to cry.

"How? With that?" I pointed at the cross-bow.

"No. I'm off home," he said, and turned his back on me. "Your effing problem."

I think he was annoyed that I was crying. I was thirteen and I was crying. And he hated that I'd killed the dawn fox, which was beautiful and meant us no harm. I'd put a stink on the cross-bow, spoiled it for him.

And now I was alone with the fox.

It seemed to have shrunk. I bent down and tried to stroke its nose, but it gave a weak snarl, and drew its lips back from its teeth. It could not lift its head. I touched its back, but there was no feeling in my hands, and I might have been touching the earth. There was none of the soft warm red that had filled my mind.

Blood oozed around the bolt. I thought it would gush if I pulled it out. I didn't know what to do. I walked away and then came back again. Snot and tears fell off my face. I saw a white plastic bag caught in the grass. I knelt and covered the fox's face with it. I thought perhaps the bag would be enough to kill it.

But one of its back legs kept moving. I cupped the little foot with my hand, and it was still. I looked around but there was still no one to help.

And so I stood up again and stepped down hard on the fox's thin skull, sobbing and crying all the time.

The memory – the thin bones breaking, the last twist of the dying fox – is in my leg even now. I can feel it the way you feel an old injury that never heals.

Without looking at what I'd done, I ran home.

And that was the end of the friendship between me and Chris Rush.

After the beck, Chris melted away. It was near the end of the semester. I didn't see him over the break, and the next semester our school merged with another, almost as hard, called St Kevin's. The classes were all jumbled, and Chris and I were split. He made new friends, tough kids, punks, skins. He never became one of the worst ones, one of the bullies, but he was on their side.

And then he got expelled for sniffing glue in the school basement. They said his pants were down and his thing was out, but I don't know about that. For a semester he hung around at the school gates, looking more and more weird. For a time I stayed to talk with him, took a drag on his cigarette. But then I heard stories about him that scared me. He had been my best friend and we'd shared everything, but now he was doing terrible things to his body, to other people's bodies.

So I stopped talking to him. To begin with I waved and laughed. And then I smiled. And then I didn't even smile any more. And then he stopped coming to the school gates, and I never saw him again.

And then Neil Johnson called, and told me that Chris was dead. He'd read about it in the local paper. The report said that Chris had been in and out of prison, mostly for stealing things or burglary. Once or twice for violence. He was in a gang with his brother, Kevin. They all shared needles. Chris got ill and wasted away.

But this wasn't meant to be a story about Chris's wasted life, but about mine. And I'm not sure what lessons it taught me. To be nice to kids like Duffy? That I should have helped Chris stay out of trouble? That he was my friend, and I could have saved him, but he was lost, and now so am I? I don't know.

I think maybe the only lesson is that sometimes when you see a firework or a fox your mind goes out into the universe, and lives with them there for a while, in glory.